Two Good Friends

For Jennifer Alice Delton (da Pudge) I love you lots.

Text copyright © 1974 by Judy Delton
Illustrations copyright © 1974 by Giulio Maestro
All rights reserved. No part of this book may be reproduced or transmitted in
any form or by any means, electronic or mechanical, including photocopying,
recording, or by any information storage and retrieval system, without
permission in writing from the publisher.
Published by Crown Publishers, Inc., 225 Park Avenue South, New York,
New York 10003 and simultaneously in Canada by
General Publishing Company Limited
CROWN is a trademark of Crown Publishers, Inc.
Manufactured in Hong Kong

Library of Congress Catalog Card Number: 73-88181
ISBN 0-517-51401-X (cloth)
ISBN 0-517-55949-8 (pbk)
10 9 8 7 6 5 4 3 2 1
First Paperback Edition, 1986

Two Good Friends

Story by Judy Delton

Pictures by Giulio Maestro

Crown Publishers, Inc.   New York

Duck had cleaned his house.

All his floors were waxed.

All his furniture was polished.

He was admiring his clean rooms
when he heard a knock at the door.

It was Bear.

"Come in," said Duck, "but first wipe your feet on the mat."

Bear wiped his feet on the mat
and went inside.

"Make yourself at home," said Duck.

"Thank you, I will," said Bear, and he
sat down in a shiny rocking chair.
Then he put his feet on Duck's table.

9

Duck reached for a newspaper and put it under Bear's feet.

"What do you have to eat?" asked Bear.

"Nothing," said Duck.

"Nothing?" asked Bear.

"Today I cleaned my house," explained
Duck. "I did not bake."

"Well, I have something," said Bear,
and he reached into his pocket and
took out two brownies.

"Bear," said Duck, "you are spilling crumbs on my floor," and he reached for another newspaper and put it under Bear's chair.

Bear looked at the newspaper.

Then he looked at the two brownies.

"Duck," he said, "you are a very good
housekeeper, but what good is a clean
house if you have nothing to eat?
Here, have a brownie."

Bear and Duck each ate a brownie and
spent the rest of the afternoon
putting a puzzle together.

The next day Duck went to visit Bear.
"Duck!" said Bear. "How nice to see
you. Come right in."

"M-m-m-m," said Duck. "What smells
so good?"

"I've been baking," said Bear, and he
pointed to two honey cakes and two
nut pies sitting on the table. "Brush
the flour off a chair and sit down."

"Bear," said Duck, "I can't sit down. My feet are stuck."

"Oh dear," said Bear. "That's the honey."

"Would you like honey cake or nut pie?"
he asked.

"Nut pie," said Duck, who had finally
managed to unstick his feet. "I've had
enough honey for one day."

"O.K.," said Bear, and he cut one piece of
nut pie for Duck and one for himself.

"May I have a plate?" asked Duck.

"The plates are dirty," said Bear.

"Well, then, may I have a fork?" asked
Duck.

"The forks are dirty too," said Bear.
He looked ashamed.

"Bear," said Duck, "how do you expect
me to eat?"

"I'm sorry," said Bear, "but today I
baked. I didn't clean the house or wash
the dishes. Maybe you can use your
wings. The pie will still taste good."

Duck and Bear each ate a piece of pie.
When Duck finished, he licked the tips
of his wings. "I must say, Bear, you
are a terrible housekeeper but your
nut pie is the best I have ever tasted."
Bear smiled. "Have another piece,"
he said.
"Gladly," said Duck, and they each ate
another piece.

The next day Bear went to Duck's house
with a surprise.
Duck was not at home but Bear went
inside anyway.

He put six raspberry muffins on the
table and wrote a note. "From Bear,"
it said. Then he went home.

When Bear walked into his house, he
was surprised. "I must be in the wrong
house," he thought. His feet did not
stick to the floor.

The dishes were washed and on the shelf.
He did not see his name where he had
written it in the flour on the table.

Instead he saw a note: "From Duck."

"I must thank Duck," thought Bear, but
just then there was a knock on the
door. It was Duck.

"Thank you for the muffins," said Duck.
"I was so surprised. And it's not even
my birthday."

"And I have never seen my house so
clean," said Bear. "I was surprised too."
"We really are good friends," said Duck.
"Yes!" cried Bear. "Let's celebrate!
Come in and have some cookies."

"But first," added Bear, "wipe your feet
on the mat."
"Of course," said Duck. And he did.